Homes
Around the World

By Maureen Dockendorf and
Sharon Jeroski

CELEBRATION PRESS
Pearson Learning Group

Dora's home is in the United States.

A home can be tall.

Oscar's home is in Bolivia.

A home can be small.

Garav's home is in Mongolia.

A home can be round.

Levi's home is in Canada.

A home can be a rectangle.

Edwin's home is in the Philippines.

A home can be on stilts.

Hannah's home is in the United Kingdom.

A home can be on water.

Caribbean

United Kingdom

Tunisia

Australia

All around the world
people live in homes.